Dear Parents,

Congratulations for choosing a fun and entertaining way to help your child learn to interact with others in pleasing, socially acceptable ways!

Children have the ability to be good, and they are often eager to please. However, they often don't understand their own egocentric or self-centered behavior. This self-centeredness often leads to misbehavior, and the misbehavior often leads to negative responses from others. All too soon, your child can be caught in a destructive cycle of negative action and reaction.

The purpose of the HELP ME BE GOOD books is to help your child break the cycle of negative action and reaction. Your child will learn how to replace misbehavior with acceptable behavior. Each HELP ME BE GOOD book is designed to do the following in an enjoyable way:

1. Define a misbehavior
2. Explain the cause of the misbehavior
3. Discuss the negative effects of the misbehavior
4. Offer suggestions for replacing the misbehavior with acceptable behavior

While it is effective to read the individual HELP ME BE GOOD books when a need arises, the series was designed to follow the normal development of young children. Consequently, presenting the books to your child in the order in which they are listed on the back cover of this book also works well.

As you and your child read the HELP ME BE GOOD books, your child will develop good behavior that will help build positive self-esteem and healthy relationships. Reading the books will also help to create a more friendly, happy atmosphere in your home. Thank you for allowing me to be a part of this exciting endeavor!

Sincerely,

Joy Berry

Joy Berry

Copyright © Joy Berry, 2022
Originally Published, 2008

All rights are reserved.

No part of this book can be duplicated or used without the prior written permission of the copyright owner, except for the use of brief quotations from the book.

For inquiries or permission requests contact the publisher.

Published by Joy Berry Enterprises
www.joyberryenterprises.com

A Help Me Be Good Book About

Being Careless

Written By Joy Berry
Illustrated By Bartholomew

Copyright © 2008 by Joy Berry

This book is about Lennie.

Reading about Lennie can help you understand and deal with **being careless**.

You are being careless when you act as if you do not care about yourself.

You are being careless when you act as if you do not care about the people and things around you.

Being careless can cause you to hurt yourself.

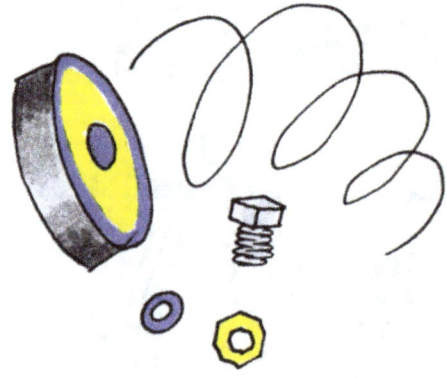

Being careless can cause you to hurt other people.

Being careless can cause you to damage or destroy things.

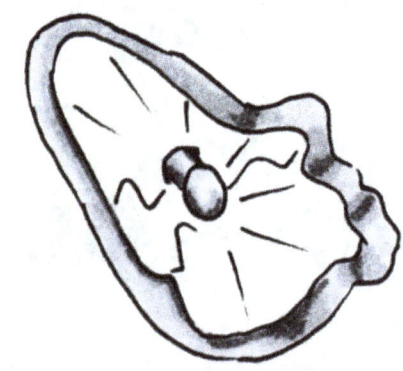

It is not good to be careless.

You need to *be careful* instead.

When you are careful, you act as if you care about yourself.

When you are careful, you act as if you care about the people and things around you.

Be careful.

Obey the rules.

Your parents usually know what you need to do to keep yourself and others safe. They usually know what you need to do to take care of the things around you.

The rules they make can help you be careful.

Be careful.

Pay attention to what you do so you will make fewer mistakes.

Be careful.

Slow down so you can avoid accidents and mistakes that happen when you hurry.

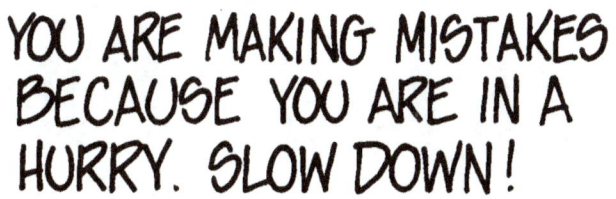

Be careful.

Watch where you are going so you can avoid tripping and bumping into things.

Be careful.

Be aware of people and things around you so you can avoid dangerous situations.

Be careful.

Avoid playing roughly so no one will get hurt and nothing will get broken.

Be careful.

Avoid playing with dangerous things so you will not hurt yourself or others.

Be careful.

Avoid playing in dangerous places so you will not hurt yourself or others.

Being careless is not good for you or the people around you.

It is better when you are careful.

Being Careless Song Lyrics
Music & Lyrics by Joy Berry, Denis Hulett & Rita Abrams

Take Care, Beware

Do you want to ride your bike real fast?
Do you want to ride your bike real fast?
If you ride your bike real fast,
Make sure no one's in your path,
If you want to ride your bike real fast.

Take care.
Beware.
Be careful what you do.
Take care.
Beware.
Take good care of you.

Do you want to go outside and play?
Do you want to go outside and play?
If you go outside and play,
Make sure where you play is safe.
If you want to go outside and play.

Take care.
Beware.
Be careful what you do.
Take care.
Beware.
Take good care of you.

Do you want to walk across the street?
Do you want to walk across the street?
If you walk across the street,
Make sure that it's clear and free,
If you want to walk across the street.

Take care.
Beware.
Be careful what you do.
Take care.
Beware.
Take good care of you.

Take care.
Beware.
Be careful what you do.
Take care.
Beware.
Take good care of you.

Careless

Well I was racing my bike,
And feeling so free.
How was I to know someone would bump into me?
Well he should've known.
And he should've seen.
What does he mean that I'm careless?

Well I was running down stairs,
To go out and play,
When momma's favorite lamp just kinda got in my way.
Well what was the lamp doing there anyway?
What does she mean I'm careless?

Look where you're going,
You gotta slow down.
You're gonna have an accident,
If you're not careful to follow the rules.
It could get unpleasant.
Not too cool.

Well I was pouring some juice,
And watching TV,
And suddenly the juice was pouring all over me.
Well who could I blame except the TV.
What do you mean I'm careless?

Look what you're doing,
You gotta slow down.
You're gonna have an accident,
If you're not careful to follow the rules.
It could get unpleasant.
Not too cool.

But now we're changing our ways.
We're changing our style.
We know now that there's more to life than just being wild.
We've had enough accidents to last us a while.
For now on we're through being careless.

Visit us on the web at www.joyberryenterprises.com!